Gabby
A Bliss Bay Romance
Kayla Love

Corner of Press

ISBN-13: 979-8-9874241-3-1

Cover Design by: Corner of Press

Artwork by: Nadezhda

Starting Over...Again!

"Hi. Sorry I'm late..." Gabby said as she hugged her cousin, Brandy, who was already seated at their usual happy hour table. Exasperated, she plopped into her seat and then placed her Bergdorf bag on the chair next to her.

"Ooh! What did you get?!" Brandy asked, excitedly. "Show me!"

"Well, I needed a little pick me up and so..." Gabby reached into the bag and pulled out the sleek black box. She opened the lid. "I got these!" She revealed the gorgeous, gold, 4-inch heels adorned with crystals. They were equal parts fierce and fabulous.

"Wow! Those are amazing! But wait...what happened that you needed a Level 10 pick me up?" Brandy stated, with a hint of worry. Over the years, the two women had developed their own cousin speak. Level 10 was reserved for the most extravagant of purchases to deal with the most epic life events.

"Let me get some bubbly in me before we go there."

"Well look at Gawd!" Brandy joked, with a little chuckle. At just that moment, their server brought over their bucket of bubbly on ice and poured two fresh glasses.

Gabby didn't wait to toast. She drained her first glass and then poured herself some more. Then took another sip.

"Okay...so the past 48 hours have been a bit of a cluster...and I'm not sure what I'm going to do," Gabby choked, tears brimming in her eyes.

"Gab! What happened?!" Brandy exclaimed. She rubbed her cousin's forearm and gave her hand a squeeze.

"Well, Dev and I broke up."

Brandy's eyes got as big as saucers. "Seriously..." she replied, sadly, empathetically, in almost a whisper.

"Yeah. That happened." She sipped some more of her bubbly. "I just couldn't do it anymore, B. It's been five. Effing. Years. And he still wouldn't move in together. I mean, damn. I know my biological clock isn't ticking because I don't want babies, but I am ready for the next level. And get this. To make it worse. This dude was planning to just go off to Boston for the summer. Never mentioned it to me."

"Wait, what? Why?" Brandy asked, incredulously.

"He got some fellowship. Like, great for him professionally, but there was no conversation. And I just knew. He wasn't trying to build a future with me. He likes me. Loves me even. But I want a real partnership and he just can't give that to me." She dabbed her eyes with a napkin. What she wasn't ready to admit, to her cousin or anyone else, was that she'd had a nagging feeling that things might end up this way.

Aww. I'm sorry."

"Thanks. So, that was *my* Sunday. And even though it was my choice, it still sucks. Here I am. At 39. Starting over again..." Gabby eked out, fighting back the floodgate of tears. "And you know I was going through it because I took a day off work! And I never do that." Gabby sighed deeply while Brandy let her speak and just listened.

On the inside, Brandy both wanted to reassure her cousin that she was a catch and everything would be okay and also that she was ready to fuck up Dev's life, if needed be, but she held her tongue and just held space. She knew that was the best thing she could do thanks to her dear friend, Ananda, a practicing therapist.

Gabby continued. "So yeah. I just felt like I needed some time to process and couldn't bear even discussing it. I barely pulled myself out of bed yesterday. But I did. Took myself to brunch. They probably thought I was bat shit crazy because I had sunglasses on the whole time…" She sipped some more of her drink. Then, I got a last minute massage , ent home ,and finally called Amaya." Amaya was Gabby's best friend. "Then I ordered takeout, drank copious amounts of bourbon, and cried myself to sleep. So yeah…I left work early today and…here we are!" She exclaimed, motioning toward her shoes.

"G…I'm so sorry. That's a lot," Brandy empathized.

"Yeah...so, we'll see. Maybe I just need a break from reality or to move or something. It's like every street I walk down has a damn memory attached to it..."

"Ugh. The absolute worst. Well, it's not moving, but...there is room in our house in Bliss Bay this summer! Could be a good distraction. I mean, it's more a sandals than stilettos vibe so you won't be able to wear those beauties," Brandy nodded toward the box of heels. "But...maybe it's just the kind of break your heart needs."

Gabby paused. Summer was quickly approaching and she didn't have any other plans. Well, not anymore. She and Dev had talked about booking a trip later that summer, but never got around to booking. *Well, why the hell not?*

"Okay. Let's do it!"

Memory Lane

"**O**kay, Skye. I'm finally off! Text me if you need anything though," Gabby said as she walked out of her office and through the lobby.

"Gabby! Go! I got you. Have fun! You deserve it," Skye, her paralegal, exclaimed.

"Thanks!" And with a wave over her shoulder, Gabby, and her overpacked weekender bag were off. She walked the five blocks from her office to Penn Station without breaking a total sweat.

Underground, she reread her text from Brandy to confirm all the things she needed to do to successfully make it out to Bliss Bay. It was a bit of a hike to get there (a train to a shuttle to a ferry), so she wanted to be sure she made it unscathed.

Gabby followed Brandy's orders and purchased her ticket from the kiosk, before walking to the liquor store between the entrances to the tracks . She grabbed two cans of cold rosé, then waited with the other beach goers for the train departure track. Shortly after, she felt a rush of air from bodies moving toward the tracks. She looked up and saw she needed to get the train on track 19 and followed suit.

Once on the train, se managed to locate an empty seat by a window. As she sat down and finally cracked open her wine, she closed her eyes and let out a sigh. Was it one of relief? Or release? Either way, she was grateful to be on her way. She needed this weekend. And as the train pulled out of the station, she shot off a quick text to Brandy.,"On my way!"

As Gabby stared out at the towns whizzing by, she couldn't help but think about how she ended up here. This most certainly was *not* where she'd thought she would be three months ago. Yet, here she was. Embarking on a new chapter. By herself. She couldn't help but think about the journey that brought her here...

***

Dev. Dev Anderson.

They'd met in the real world, much to her surprise, given most of the dating world was so focused on apps. It was a random Thursday night out in February. She'd not even been in the city a full year after moving up from Atlanta after yet another breakup. She'd stopped at a bar by the office for a drink with Skye. Gabby stayed to finish her whiskey after Skye left for her train to New Jersey. Right before she was ready to close out and head home, a handsome gentleman with thick, black hair and a killer smile sat next to her at the bar and struck up a conversation.

Dev Anderson was also new-ish to the city after living in Houston. He worked in commercial real estate development, lived downtown, and also liked his whiskey neat. That was enough for her to give him her phone number when he asked. She'd later learn he was three years younger, which normally would have been a dealbreaker since, until now, Gabby had exclusively dated older men. She had also never dated a non-Black man, but new city, new approach. She was open to whatever New York had to offer. Much to her delight, he sent a text before she even made it home. In the back seat of a cab, a smile crept across her face as she responded and accepted a date for Sunday.

Their first date was sweet. Lunch and lattes at Eataly followed by a stroll through Madison Square Park. He left her with a brief kiss and a plan for a second date for midweek.

Their second date was spicy. After a few days of sending flirtatious text messages and funny memes, they met for cocktails at a speakeasy she'd been dying to try! Somehow Dev worked his magic and got them reservations for the dark and sultry basement bar.

They talked about everything. Jobs. Family. Friends. Life. It was everything she'd always desired - and wouldn't have had if she wasn't open to something new! As he spoke, his hand took residence on her knee, which was exposed below the hemline of her sweater dress. Her heart went pitter-patter. She attempted to focus on his words and hold eye contact with his soul-searching brown eyes. But her eyes couldn't help darting away to focus on his full lips that she couldn't wait to kiss again.

Her ears perked up as she took another sip of her gin cocktail. He shared how he had other aspirations and didn't want children. It was so rare for her to find someone else who didn't want to procreate. She was intrigued!

"But I'm not against the practice activities!" he said with a wink.

This time her nether regions went pitter-patter. She was never much of a rules girl, but she did try to pace things out a bit. She wasn't sure how much pacing she would be able to do with Dev as her thoughts easily wandered to bedroom behavior.

Cocktails to crudo to kisses outside of the restaurant. Gabby didn't give a shit who passed by or shouted "get a room." She was thoroughly enjoying her lip lock with Dev. When she finally came up for air, he hailed her a cab and she was on cloud nine the entire ride home. They'd already made plans for Saturday night. *Would that be 'the night'?*

And So it Begins

The third date was indeed, THE NIGHT. Delicious dinner. Divine dessert. Copious amounts of wine. A nightcap in a small, dark, and sexy bar where Dev whispered into Gabby's ear and sent tingles down her spine. Gabby couldn't wait! She took the lead, cupped Dev's face and planted a soft, deep kiss on his lips leaving the taste and heat of whiskey behind. His hand made its way to her thigh. She placed her hand on top of his and interlaced her fingers with his. More kisses. The tingles had moved from her spine to between her legs. She didn't think she was going to be able to hold out much longer. And she didn't.

Moments later Dev asked, "You want to get outta here?"

Gabby nodded in agreement. Dev grabbed her hand and led her through the swarm of bumping bodies and pulsating beats to the sidewalk where he hailed a cab.

"West 10th and Weehawken."

As the cab driver navigated the city streets, Dev navigated Gabby's body. His hands moved from lightly gripping the back of her neck as he kissed her passionately to grazing her nipples with his fingers. A small moan escaped her mouth. She responded by lightly running her manicured nails up and down his back.

Their bodies lurched as the cab driver swerved around a car. They giggled and then returned to their make out session oblivious to the bright lights and city sounds. By the time they pulled up to Dev's place, his hands were under her dress and rubbing her ass as Gabby was teasing him by tugging at his zipper. They could hardly contain themselves. Dev pulled out two twenties and handed them to the driver as they emerged from the cab. It was a race to open up his building door and then the door to his bachelor pad, which, thankfully, met her standards for cleanliness and grown-upness.

Before she had a minute to think further, Dev had wrapped his arms around her and was kissing her neck. She sighed as she grabbed his face to kiss him some more. When they came up for air, he clasped her hand and guided her toward the bedroom where it was a mad dash to remove their clothing. Gabby pulled Dev's shirt off over his head revealing the fact that he definitely was working on his fitness in the gym. She admired his physique for a moment before kissing him some more. With one hand, he gently moved her hair out of the way to use his other hand to reveal her zipper. She turned around and let Dev's fingers slowly, yet nimbly pull the zipper down placing kisses along her spine, only pausing to unhook her bra. Her dress eventually dropped to the floor revealing her thong.

Dev turned her around. His eyes lustfully looked her up and down before hoisting her up on his waist and up against the wall...

The next morning in the cab, Gabby sent a text dishing all the details to Brandy and Amaya. She ended the series of texts with "I really like him! Wish me luck!"

Turns out, luck was on her side! After many more dates, a few weeks later, Dev made it official and he and Gabby effortlessly became a couple. The first three years of were amazing! They integrated well Into each other's lives. Met each other's friends. Celebrated each other's birthdays. The typical milestones in a relationship. They would get in little tiffs, of course, but never any epic fights. She wasn't in a rush. But by the fourth year, Gabby was getting antsy and ready for them to take the next step. Any next step. Moving in together. Getting engaged. Something. She hinted at the conversation, but hesitated to directly say anything. The last time she'd done that, it ended her relationship and sparked her move to New York City.

Then, the first Friday in January, Gabby opened her apartment door as she came home from work. As she kicked her shoes off at the door, she noticed an envelope. She picked it up and opened it. It was her lease renewal. She immediately poured herself some whiskey and flopped down on the couch. She was going to need a little liquid courage to plan how she was going to bring up the idea of moving in together with Dev...

The next day, Gabby found herself standing outside of Dev's building, annoyed, as she rang the buzzer. They were headed to a friend's place for a game night. She pulled her coat closed as the winter evening's chill ran through her body.

"Damn, Dev. Come on!" she muttered with a shudder.

If they lived together, or hell, if she had a key, this wouldn't be an issue. She buzzed again. A moment later the door clicked open. She climbed the steps to the second floor where Dev's apartment door was cracked open. She walked in to Dev shirtless and in jeans.

"Impatient much?" he teased, giving her a peck on the cheek. She lightly punched his shoulder.

"It's fucking cold out! If I had a key I wouldn't have had to wait," she said with a smirk. He didn't say anything for a beat too long so she quickly interjected, "ETA?"

"Give me 5."

She knew that meant 10, so she grabbed a glass out of the cabinet and poured herself a nip of the bourbon he already had on the counter. She took her glass to the couch and began reciting her script in her head. A few minutes later he was ready and they hopped in a cab for the 20 minute ride to the Lower East Side.

"So I was thinking..." Gabby started as the cab turned left on Houston. Dev looked up from his phone, eyebrows raised. "So, I got my lease renewal notice and I was thinking maybe we should finally think about moving in together. I mean. I don't know when you renew but we could figure something out if the timing doesn't work. I mean I could put stuff in storage or..." Gabby rambled.

"Oh..." Dev trailed off.

Shit. That wasn't what she was expecting.

"Well, I, umm, I just renewed a couple weeks ago. And I guess...I mean, umm..."

With every stutter, Gabby's insides cringed. *Dammit!*

"I mean, I figured we liked having our own spaces and all..."

"No. No. It's okay. It's fine," Gabby eked out as she turned to face the window, tears stinging her eyes.

Don't you dare fucking cry! Her inside voice yelled. She took a deep breath and sighed heavily. She felt Dev move his hand on her thigh, she reluctantly placed hers on top of his, but couldn't look him in the eye.

The ten minutes remaining in the ride felt like an eternity. But it gave Gabby time to figure out how she was going to put on a happy face at this party with their couple friends, most of whom already lived together, including the ones who had been together less time!

When they arrived, Dev grabbed her hand and led them toward the door. Gabby stayed silent pulling herself together.

"Can we chat later, babe?" Dev asked.

Gabby nodded as she choked back tears. She took a deep breath and rallied for the party.

Know When to Fold 'Em

The party ended up being fine. Gabby even contemplated changing her career to actress after the performance she put on. It was like they were the happiest couple and all was well in the world. She was exhausted by 12:30 when they finally said their goodbyes.

The next morning, they attempted to have the conversation.

"Listen, I..." Dev started the same time Gabby began, "I guess I'm just..."

"You go," Gabby said.

"GG. You know I love you," he said, grabbing her hand, and using his nickname for her. GG. For Gabrielle Giselle. Her first and middle names. "And I'm sorry you are upset. I'm just...not ready. For that...I mean, I know we've been together a while, but I thought you liked us having our own places and independence. I guess I just thought things are so good as they are. It's just..." He trailed off.

"It made sense to me," Gabby interjected. "I mean, because things are so good. Why wouldn't we?!" she said with hot tears pricking her eyes.

"I just...need more time. Can we make that work?"

Gabby was silent for a beat. She wanted to take this step, but she wasn't willing to break up over it. Not yet at least. But she also wasn't going to wait forever. She just didn't feel like having that conversation right now.

"Yeah. We can."

Gabby tried. For a couple of months. She was hopeful that with a little more time they could revisit the conversation. She'd gone month to month on her lease just in case. But as winter turned into spring and their fifth anniversary was approaching, Gabby knew she had to put on her big girl panties and put a stake in the ground.

It was a sunny Sunday morning and the couple went to a brunch spot around the corner from Gabby's. After a few sips of her Bloody Mary, Gabby was feeling bold enough to broach the topic when Dev said, "I want to talk to you about something."

This is it! He's come to the idea on his own. All he needed was a little time!

She tried not to look too eager.

"So, I didn't say anything before because I wasn't sure I would get in, and applied on a whim after my mentor told me about it, but..." Dev slid a paper across the table toward Gabby. "I got into the Harvard Fellowship!"

Gabby was stunned. So stunned she couldn't even be excited or control her response. She spat out, "Hold up. You knew there was a possibility you'd be moving and you didn't say jack shit until now?"

Dev's face said it all. He was so excited that he didn't think through this potential response. "Well. I figured we'd cross that bridge when it came time..." he replied sheepishly.

"Another Bloody Mary?!" the chipper waitress asked as she broke the intensity of the moment.

"I'm good," Gabby said tersely. She wanted to sprint out of the restaurant and back to the safety and comfort of her apartment. But her stomach was growling and she wanted to eat her bacon first.

"I will take one," Dev stammered.

The waitress left and the thick tension between Gabby and Dev remained. Gabby silently sipped her drink. Knowing her nearly five years now, Dev knew to shut the fuck up. He might not always think ahead to avoid confrontation but knew damn well what to do when Gabby was quiet as a church mouse pissed.

After what felt like a silent eternity, hot plates of eggs, bacon, potatoes, and French toast were placed on the table in front of them. Gabby nibbled on a piece of crispy bacon. She didn't have much appetite left. She wanted to take her food and go. The waitress passed by.

"Excuse me! Can I get a box, please?"

Gabby cut their usual shared French toast in half and placed it in the box with the rest of her food.

"I can't do this anymore. I love you, but I can't do it," Gabby declared.

"GG, seriously?"

She stood up, picked up her box, and replied, "Seriously."

***

"Harbor Side Station!" the conductor yelled, snapping Gabby out of her reminiscing.

She gathered up her belongings. She felt the flutter of butterflies in her stomach. She wasn't sure if it was the wine or this adventure feeling like the first day of school. After all, she only knew Brandy and Jalen. She'd met a friend or two at their parties, but was always with Dev, so didn't ever pay that close of attention. As she stepped onto the platform, a whiff of salt air immediately put her at ease.

A few minutes later, she found herself on the top of the ferry observing the other beachgoers from behind her Tom Ford sunglasses. Groups of girlfriends gabbing and gossiping about their weeks, insulated cups of alcohol in hand. Guys with coolers doing the same. It was only the stolen glances at the smattering of couples that caused hot tears to form in her eyes. She quickly dabbed them and averted her gaze to the wide expanse of ocean.

Starting over sucked, but she was determined to make the most of it. *What's that expression? The only way to get over someone is to get under someone else.* That was going to be her plan. And from what she'd heard from Brandy, there would be ample opportunities to make that happen. Yup. This summer was going to be all about her. She was going to trade her tears for triumph. No crying, only conquests. And as the ferry approached the dock, to Bliss Bay she thought, *here goes nothing!*

Guess Who's Coming to Dinner?

G abby followed Brandy's detailed text on how to get to the house. "Follow the path past The Bungalow. After the second set of cross streets, it will be the 5th house on the left. Door will be open!" She tapped on the door as she pushed it open.

"Hellooo!" Gabby called out.

"Gab!" she heard Brandy's voice from down the hall. A moment later, she saw her cousin appear, looking relaxed, curls atop of her head, wearing a turquoise bikini top and denim shorts. Brandy greeted her with a tight hug. "I'm so glad you're here!"

"Me too. Where should I put my stuff?"

"Of course, of course. Let me get you settled." Brandy walked Gabby down the hall to the simple room with two twin beds. "Here's your room! You'll be sharing with Meena. You'll love her! Bathroom is across the hall. Linens are in the closet in there," Brandy said as she pointed and led the way back down the hall and toward the deck outdoors. "Washer and dryer in there, beach chairs, umbrellas, and things in there. Outdoor shower over there. And obviously, there's the outdoor dining area and grill." Gabby took it all in and nodded.

Back in the house, Brandy was showing Gabby the kitchen when a booming voice shouted, "Drankkksss!" It was Brandy's friend Jeremy, who was now in a neighboring house since Brandy decided to do this house with Jalen. He placed a pitcher and some cups on the counter.

"Hey Jeremy!" Brandy exclaimed as she gave him a hug. "You remember my cousin Gabby from the Halloween party, right?"

"Yeah. Hey. Nice to see you again!" Jeremy said, warmly, and offered Gabby a hug. Then, he grabbed a cup, poured some of the liquid from the pitcher in it, and handed it to Gabby. "For you!!"

"Thanks!" She wasn't one to refuse a cocktail.

"Sunset Punch. My new signature drink."

Gabby took a sip. "It's delicious!" she replied, as she drained the rest of the drink.

"Okay! Let's get this party started," Jeremy shouted.

And they did. Jalen appeared from the back room and turned on some tunes before firing up the grill. Gabby helped Brandy make a cheese plate. Jeremy made another batch of drinks. Other house members and neighbors trickled in. Everyone was really nice and Gabby felt comfortable and at ease.

Gabby felt happily tipsy as she sat down at the table for dinner with the crew that had assembled. She looked down to fill up her glass with some wine and when she looked up, she locked eyes with a tall, attractive man with rich caramel colored skin. *Now there's a tree I'd like to climb...*

The hottie was introduced as Victor. And when he shook Gabby's hand, she felt an electric jolt she hadn't felt in quite some time. She learned he was a friend of Ryan, one of their housemates, and was a guest for the weekend since Ethan couldn't make it. It took everything inside Gabby not to turn into a middle school girl scribbling their names on a napkin. She managed to play it cool and interact like the sophisticated 39 year old she was - and without spilling any of her wine or anything else equally embarrassing.

After they cleaned up dinner, Jeremy and some of the neighbor friends headed back to their place with the promise of seeing everyone out at The Sand Dollar. The smaller group: Brandy and Jalen, Ty and Tiffany, Gabby, Victor, Ryan, and Meena decided to have some more drinks and play a game. She ended up across the table from Victor. Not only did he have captivating eyes, but also a stellar smile. *Can he see me blushing?*

Ryan brought over a mixing bowl, some pens, and some paper and placed it on the table next to the bottle of wine and a couple of beers that Ty had placed on the table.

"Celebrity!" Ryan exclaimed. "Everyone knows how it works?"

They did. Everyone got to writing out five names on the slips of paper and started the game. Lots of laughs were had. The game was close. Gabby was up and needed to get 4 correct for the ladies to win. On the last clue with eight seconds to go, Gabby grabbed the bottle of wine, held her ear, and mimed singing.

"Mariah Carey!" Brandy shouted. Cheers erupted as the women went wild at their win!

"Good game, good game," Jalen said, grabbing Brandy in a hug, only slightly salty because of his competitive nature.

Victor approached Gabby with his hand raised for a high five. She reciprocated and felt his hand grasp hers just a bit as he said, "Well played."

"Thanks," she replied with a subtle bat of the eyes. All this wine had her feeling a little frisky.

The moment was broken by Brandy announcing they were going to get ready for the bar.

Dammit, cousin!

She knew Brandy would never intentionally cock block her, so maybe she didn't notice a vibe between them.

Maybe this is one sided? I should chill.

After consuming copious amounts of wine, Gabby was not her sharpest, so she wasn't sure if she had just concocted what she was feeling toward Victor. For now, she'd just focus on getting cute for the bar.

It felt like the glory days of college. Music blasting. Drinks flowing. Putting on makeup in the mirror with a friend. Giving advice on evening outfits. Gabby had selected a long, flowy, emerald green sundress that popped against her glowing skin. As the crew exited the house toward the bar, she couldn't help but notice Victor eyeing her just a bit. So maybe she wasn't so off.

The night at the bar was typical for a Friday night in Bliss Bay. Folks filed in and out. Some danced to the tunes from the jukebox. Some played pool. Some just talked for hours over their drinks. As the hours passed and the work week caught up with them, folks dropped like flies and made their way back to their houses.

And then there were five. Gabby, Brandy, Jalen, Meena, and...Victor.

At the round table outside the bar, Gabby was seated between Brandy and Victor. Usually she was great at making conversation, but her little crush on Victor made her feel like a teenage girl again. She needed alcohol to lubricate this situation.

"Anybody need a drink?" Gabby asked as she stood. Everyone said they were content with what they had, except Victor, who stood and said he'd venture in with Gabby. She felt a flutter in her stomach. As Victor let her pass to follow her in, his hand ever so gently grazed the small of her back and that flutter flew south.

Will They or Won't They?

At the bar, Gabby asked for a whiskey neat.

"Bold choice," Victor stated, as he looked at Gabby.

"Bold woman," she quickly retorted back with a wink. *There it was!* Coming back into the arena...it's Gabby's mojo!

"I'll have the same," he said, as the bartender looked to him for his choice.

While they waited for their pours in plastic cups, Victor asked, "So what brought you here this weekend? You a regular?"

"Not quite. But I guess I will be by the end of summer. I have a share for this summer, but it's my first season. What about you?"

"Oh it's my first time as well. But not for the full summer. Just a guest for the weekend.

Ryan's a buddy of mine and I didn't have any plans so jumped at the chance."

"Cool. Brandy's my cousin. She knew I was looking to do more than stay in the city this summer so invited me to join. So far, so good!"

"Yeah. I'm excited to hit the beach tomorrow, too."

"Same."

The cups of brown liquor were placed in front of them and Victor quickly handed the bartender some cash for their drinks.

"Thank you," Gabby said, ever so slightly batting her eyelashes.

"No problem," Victor answered. "Shall we?"

They walked back to the table where Brandy and Jalen were clearly people watching and whispering.

"Where's Meena?" Gabby asked as she found her way back to her seat.

Brandy giggled. "Girl, she's gone."

"That quick? What happened?" Gabby inquired.

"Oh she saw Bliss Bay Bae! And it was a wrap!"

"Bliss Bay Bay?" Victor interjected.

"Yes. Like her boo. Her summer boo."

"Ohhhhh," Gabby and Victor responded in understanding.

"Yup. So if you see one of the beach blankets is missing, you know why!" Brandy exclaimed as she and Jalen chuckled.

"Catch up, y'all," Jalen added. He could see in their eyes that Gabby and Victor were perplexed. "You realize we're in close quarters, right? So rather than kick a roommate out, folks take a blanket to the beach as another option."

"Ohhhhh," again, Victor and Gabby responded in unison.

"Now there are pros and cons to that!" Brandy chimed in.

I can imagine. Like places where sand doesn't need to be!" Gabby replied.

"True. True. And also, rumor has it some people were once spotted from afar because it was a full moon. A full moon spotted under the full moon!" Brandy exclaimed as she smacked her hand on the table cracking herself up.

"Well damn!" Victor replied.

Jalen held his hands up. "Hey. We don't judge. Some folks like to be close to nature."

"That's one way to explore the outdoors!" Victor added.

"Well now we know!" Gabby added. She took a sip of her whiskey and wondered. She'd only ever enjoyed sex on the beach as a cocktail. Would she get down like that? It wasn't her usual speed, but hell. This summer was for adventures and experiences. Would it be with Victor? There seemed to be some kind of vibe, but she couldn't totally tell. It had been years since she'd been interested in someone new. At this point, she was tired and tipsy and needed some sleep. It had been a day.

Gabby finished her last sip before announcing, "Okay team. I gotta call it."

The rest of the group agreed and the foursome walked back to their house.

Gabby and Victor were sharing the same bathroom so they did the little dance of moving out of each other's way as they washed their faces and brushed their teeth. Something about the intimate nature of being seen makeupless and with toothpaste foaming in her mouth made her a little wistful. Instead of the butterflies she felt earlier, this felt more like a tugging at her heart. A longing. Part of her wanted to ask Victor into her room, where she knew Meena's bed was empty. Not to tear off his clothes as she originally thought. But instead just to hold her. Even though her breakup was the right decision - and her decision - she still wasn't over that empty space in her bed. She chalked all of these thoughts and feelings up to the whiskey running through her veins. She just needed sleep. She said goodnight and then made her way to the quiet of her room. She knocked out as soon as her head hit the pillow.

Making Contact

The next morning, Gabby was awakened by the smell of coffee and bacon and she desperately wanted both. She rolled out of bed to put herself together enough to join the crew in the kitchen and noticed a light trail of sand from the door to the bed where Meena was sound asleep, wearing a towel, half under her sheet. She must have been worn out from her night of fun! Gabby would learn later that Meena wore that towel not only on the way home, but also to a party since somehow her dress went missing, but not her towel.

In the kitchen, Jalen was making bacon and Brandy was carefully filling glasses with bubbly.

"Hey G!" Brandy said. "Sleep well?"

"Yeah. I did."

"Did Meena make it back?" Brandy asked with a chuckle as she handed Gabby her breakfast cocktail how she liked it. Heavy on the bubbles. Light on the juice. Grapefruit, not orange.

"Thanks, B. And she did. With a trail of sand!" Gabby didn't notice anyone else in the kitchen. In particular, Victor. But she decided to play it cool and ask about everyone. "So where is everyone else?"

"Oh Ty and Tiff went on an early bike ride. Babe, have you seen Ryan or Victor?" Brandy asked.

Jalen turned around from the pan of bacon. "I'm certain Ryan's asleep. He lives for a day to sleep in. Not sure about Victor."

Okay. So maybe I have time to get cuter than this morning look before I see him again.

That went out the door when a moment later, Victor walked in shirtless, sweat glistening on his Adonis-like body. It took everything in Gabby's power not to drool. Instead she took a healthy sip of her drink before greeting Victor.

"Hey Victor!" Gabby stated. "You're up and at 'em early!"

"Yeah," he said as he walked toward the fridge to grab a bottle of water. "I'm training for a half marathon, so I needed to get those miles in before it got too hot."

"Nice! Can I interest you in a mimosa?"

"Y'all really get after it! Let me rinse off, but yes. Thanks." Victor said with a wink as he headed toward the shower.

Gabby hoped Brandy didn't see her face flush. She wasn't quite ready to show her cards. She focused on her task at hand. She grabbed the bottle of bubbly and poured it in a glass, which she handed to Victor when he returned.

The other housemates eventually returned from excursions or sleepily made their way to the kitchen for breakfast before the group readied themselves for a day at the beach. Gabby was excited to give her new swimsuit a whirl. She felt good. Bold. Sexy. *Ain't no way he's gonna be able to resist me after this!*

And she was right! Down on the beach, she removed her cover up and behind her sunglasses, she could see Victor's eyes damn near pop out of his head! And it couldn't have been a coincidence that he just happened to have his beach chair next to hers. He wasn't overtly flirting, but Gabby was perceptive and noticed how he would find ways to make contact. A light touch on her knee while telling a story. Fingertips grazing as he handed her a cold seltzer. Tucking an errant curl behind her ear. Each one sent electric shocks throughout her body. Her lady parts were pulsating.

The tension between them continued to mount as afternoon turned toward evening. Gabby had volunteered to cook dinner and Victor offered to be her sous chef. While the rest of the crew stayed down on the beach, Gabby savored her alone time with Victor while they listened to a summer jams playlist and sipped wine as they shucked corn, chopped veggies, and set the table for dinner. More than once their bodies lightly brushed against each other as they moved around the kitchen.

She didn't know if it was the wine, the warm breeze, or the wink Victor gave her, but when she turned toward the fridge and found herself face to face with him, something came over her. She cut the tension by planting a soft, warm kiss on his lips.

Victor reciprocated the kiss with passion, his hands cupping the sides of Gabby's face as he leaned into it.

Ting. Ting. Ting.

The moment was interrupted by the sound of the alarm Victor had set for the corn on the grill. He continued kissing Gabby for another beat before pulling away to grab the phone and turn off the disruptive noise.

"Guess you better check on the corn," Gabby said, slightly breathless and flushed.

"I guess I better," he said while maintaining full eye contact. It was clear he was deciding between having perfectly grilled corn or another perfect kiss with Gabby.

"Nope. No, no, no!" Brandy's voice startled them both as she opened the screen door.

"I'm going to go check on the corn," Victor announced.

"Great! Thank you," Gabby replied as if they weren't just lip locked a few seconds before.

Brandy came around the corner with Jalen behind her. "Gab, help me out here. This man is trying to tell me that 7-11 is better than Wawa! Is he for real? It's incomparable. Can you get hoagies at 7-11? Can you get legit good coffee there? No and no."

"But the Slurpees, B. You can't get them at Wawa." Jalen replied

"When was the last time you had a Slurpee, sir?!" Brandy teased, as she poked Jalen in the ribs.

"Okay, okay. You got me," Jalen stated as he grabbed Brandy from behind and snuggled her. She shrieked.

Gabby felt a little tug at her heart. She missed being in a relationship. She hoped she would be again one day, but for now, she was determined to focus on fun.

"Okay, Gab. How can I help? I'm going to take a quick shower and then I'm all yours. Everyone else should be back up soon," Brandy inquired.

"I think we're almost ready. Victor was helpful on the grill so maybe just getting the drinks ready.

Okay. Back in a few!"

Sex on the Beach

G abby didn't think her cousin had any inkling of what had gone down in the kitchen a mere minutes before. *And definitely not what was going up!* There was no guessing about Victor's interest anymore. Gabby felt it. Literally.

Before long the group was assembled at the table for another delicious meal which everyone promptly devoured. In fact, they were so into the food that no one noticed Victor gripping Gabby's knee under the table nor her bare foot lightly stroking his calf.

Post dinner, the crew ended up back at The Sand Dollar where Victor and Gabby continued to give each other knowing glances. They had an understanding they were going to keep this interlude, whenever it happened, undercover. When they realized that the couples were engaged in deep conversation at a table, Meena was making out with Bliss Bay Bae outside the bar, and Ryan was chatting up a cutie in the corner, it was their chance. They did everything but sprint out the side door and sneak back to the house.

They stumbled into the room Victor was sharing with Ryan. He kicked the door closed behind him as he ran his fingers through her hair and pulled her face toward his. He planted kisses on her lips and then down on her neck. She gasped in delight before returning the favor. She lightly nibbled on his neck. He moaned and pulled her closer. He only pulled away to reach for the hem of her cover up and pull it up over her head revealing her lime green halter bikini top. It was at that moment Gabby realized she never got "dressed" for the night. She was still in her swimsuit and cover up and had just thrown on jean shorts. She never did her hair or put on makeup. And this man was still into her in her natural state. That, in and of itself, was a turn on.

Just as she went to grab for Victor's swim trunks, they heard noises outside the window and both froze. It was voices!

They listened and realized it was Ty and Tiffany coming back to the house to grab Tiffany's jacket because she was cold. A moment later, they heard the screen door shut and the couple's voices diminish as they left the house.

"That was close!" Gabby whispered.

"It was," Victor replied, catching his breath. "Should we take this to the beach?"

"Let's do it!"

Gabby grabbed the blanket and a sheet from the closet. They tiptoed out of the house and giddily pranced down the path toward the beach. They set up shop about halfway between the edge of the path and the ocean and managed not to get sand all over the place. They sat side by side on the blanket, the glow of the moon glistening on their sun kissed skin, the waves crashing ahead. It was intoxicating! Just as Gabby was soaking it all in, Victor leaned over to kiss her and restart what they began back at the house.

He laid her on the blanket and continued kissing Gabby who was glad to oblige. Her body had desperately missed this kind of touch. She couldn't get enough fast enough. So when Victor asked, "You good?" she enthusiastically replied, "Yes! Keep going!"

And he did.

He moved down from her neck to her cleavage where he realized her bikini top was in the way. He lifted her up with one hand and used his other to undo her top from the back freeing her full breasts. She responded by grabbing his shirt and pulling it over his head so they would both be bare chested. Their hands continued to explore each other's bodies until Gabby decided to take things even further to Victor's delight and pleasure.

As he laid on his back, she tugged at the waistband of his swim shorts, removing them rapidly and tossing them to the side. She was impressed with what was revealed and used her hands to taunt and tease him. She enjoyed the feeling of being in control of his moans and groans and exclamations of "Dios Mio!" And finally, when she was ready and about to explode, she shimmied out of her bottoms, lowered on top of him, and took control of her own satisfaction.

When they finally caught their breath, they retrieved their scattered belongings, folded up the blanket, and walked back to the house.

"Are you as shocked as me that we aren't more sandy than this?!" Gabby whispered and chuckled.

"For real," Victor added in his own hushed tone. "That still would have been worth it." Gabby could see his excited eyebrow raise out of the corner of her eye.

"I wonder if they're back from the bar yet," Gabby wondered as they approached the house.

"What time is it even? I didn't even bring my phone."

Me either!"

The house was dark, except for the porch light. They brushed off the sand and kicked off their flip flops by the door and walked in.

"Midnight," Gabby declared as she saw the clock. "Hmm. Brandy and Jalen could be here asleep or out knowing them."

"Yeah. I'm guessing Ryan is still making moves on that girl from the bar if I know him!"

"Well good for him for getting after it!" Gabby exclaimed. "And what I'm about to get after...is my bed. I'm gonna sleep good tonight!"

"You and me both. Thanks for a great night." Victor planted a soft kiss on Gabby's lips.

And before either of them could get any ideas about ravaging each other on the kitchen island, they both slipped off to their respective rooms.

Summer Lovin'

The next morning, Gabby was up early and felt like a new woman. Last night was exactly what she needed. In the kitchen, she ran into Brandy who was also, surprisingly, up early.

"Oh hey B," Gabby greeted her cousin.

"Morning! Where'd you end up last night?" Brandy asked as she scooped coffee grounds into the machine. Gabby froze for a beat before quickly responding, "Oh I just went to The Bungalow."

Brandy paused, gave her cousin the side eye, and said "Now I know you're lying! Because I ended up there and you were nowhere to be seen. Get your flip flops. We're going on an outing."

Gabby knew she was caught so she followed orders. Brandy started the coffee since she knew Jalen would want some when he got up.

She sent him a quick text on the way out to let him know and then led Gabby down toward the mini market where they could grab iced coffees and gossip on the dock.

When they were out of earshot of the house, Brandy exclaimed, "Okay spill it!"

"Well..." Gabby started. "I got back on the horse if that was what you were wondering!"

"Yassss! Good for you. Victor I'm assuming..."

"How did you know?!

"Well, you just told me. But also, you know I'm observant. And when J and I got home last night I just happened to see your flip flops and a pair I assumed were his when we came in. The lights were all out so I wasn't certain, but I had a feeling!"

"Damn. You catch everything! But yeah. It was good. Fun. Exactly what I needed."

"Awww good G! Now you know I'm gonna want a few more details than that. But also, do you think you'll see him again back in the city?!"

"Um, maybe? We didn't discuss it. But I don't think it was like that. I think it was an understanding that it was a fun moment and maybe that's all. Don't get me wrong. He's a great guy, but I'm not ready for anything serious again and I'm totally okay if all it was was what it was."

"I hear you," Brandy acknowledged. "But once we get these iced coffees I want to hear the juicy stuff! Because it sounds like you got over someone by getting under someone else...mmm hm-mmm."

"Well, not just under, but also over, on the side..." Gabby replied.

"Girlllllll....get it, get it!" Brandy answered while doing a body roll as she opened the door to the mini market.

After their coffee and gossip session, the cousins went back to the house where it was another standard beach day before they all packed up to take an evening ferry back to land and back to reality. Gabby and Victor parted ways on friendly terms and left their "sand" at the beach. It was actually refreshing to Gabby that there was no forcing a phone number exchange or pretending they would make plans in the city. If their paths crossed again, great. If not, it was a mutually fun summer experience.

And that was how the next two months progressed for Gabby. Beach and boys. Fun and flings. Rinse and repeat.

There was Belmont Brent she met watching the horse race at The Bungalow. He made up for her $20 loss on 'Angel's Advocate' by making out with her outside the bar.

Then there was Cook Off Chris. They bonded over his winning lamb burger and her winning pomegranate margarita in the hotly contested Bliss Bay competition. Margaritas all day, plus one too many Modelos at The Sand Dollar ended up with them fooling around in the hot tub at his house.

And then there was the one Brandy liked to call The Toddler. He was of legal and consenting age, but a solid 15 years younger — a baby compared to Gabby. He showed up in a captain's uniform to the Naughty Nautical party their neighbors had. When it got too hot, they went to the beach to cool off. But after some sexy skinny dipping, she ended up teaching him a few things on that lifeguard stand!

GABBY

From the outside looking in, it looked like Project Get Over Dev was working, but no one knew the two big secrets Gabby was keeping.

An Unexpected Surprise

It was early August, and yes, Gabby was having fun. As a self proclaimed serial monogamist, she had never really been single for very long, so she hadn't had much chance to have fun and explore men she never would have considered with no strings attached. But, the novelty was already wearing off and she was finding herself depressed.

No one, not even Brandy or Amaya, knew the extent of the despair Gabby felt at her current state of affairs. They didn't know how many Sunday nights she returned home trading the salt water for salty tears of sadness that soaked her pillow. Maybe it was her pride. She couldn't stand admitting that she had to start over again. Maybe she despised having to be vulnerable and just didn't want to admit how demoralized she was by the fact that she was 39, the clock ticking toward her 40th birthday, and back at square one. With no prospects in sight. It was discouraging.

She missed Dev, but not as much as the idea of being in a relationship. Someone to snuggle with on a Friday night. To tackle the crossword with on a Sunday morning. To take as a plus one to the office holiday party. They just didn't have the same pop on their own.

The only glimmer of hope was Gabby's other secret. While she'd been enjoying her work, she was ready for a new professional challenge and the opportunities were abundant. In Los Angeles that is. She'd been making connections with colleagues out there and had even planned a trip to explore her options.

The Monday before Labor Day, Gabby found herself at JFK Airport bright and early headed to L.A. for a few days. As she waited at the gate for her flight, out of the corner of her eye, she noticed a handsome guy with warm brown skin looking her way. She didn't think much of it.

"Gabrielle Alexander. Can we see you at the counter?"

Gabby grabbed her bag and walked up to the counter.

"Ma'am. Here's a new ticket for you. You've been upgraded. Enjoy!"

"Thank you!" Gabby was excited. This was an unexpected surprise and good omen for her trip.

Shortly after, they called for first class passengers, so she made her way onto the plane. After putting up her bags, she made herself cozy in her window seat with all her essentials. She was so preoccupied with getting settled, it wasn't until she was buckled in and the flight attendant asked for her drink order that she noticed the handsome guy from before was waiting to sit in the seat next to her.

Is it me or does he look familiar? Do I know him?

It wasn't the first time she thought she knew someone she saw. Although last time it was a B-list actor and not someone she knew personally. She smiled and then looked back at her phone.

"Your mimosa, ma'am," the flight attendant said as she handed her the pre-flight beverage and a napkin.

"Thank you!"

"Gabrielle?" he asked.

"Uh...yes?" she said curiously as she turned her face toward him and actually saw the features of his face and it registered.

Oh. My. God.

"Dante?! Dante Clark?!"

"It's me," he replied. "I thought it was a long shot that it was you, but then I heard them call your name at the gate. What's it been? Twenty years?"

"Yeah, something like that." Gabby took a sip of her drink. "So do you live in New York? L.A.? Catch me up on the past 20 years?"

Over the course of the flight, Gabby and Dante caught up on life. Since they last saw each other in the Heathrow airport after their semester in London, a lot of life had happened. And because this was during the pre-social media era, and they each had significant others back at their respective colleges, they didn't end up staying in touch.

Gabby learned that after study abroad, Dante finished undergrad at Wake Forest, then eventually made his way to D.C. for business school at Georgetown, right after Gabby had left the area for law school at Emory. Right when she moved to New York, he moved to Atlanta for a job, and to be near his parents who had retired there after a life of traveling in the Army. It was almost as if he was following, and just missing, her. Until now.

During that time he'd also broken up, gotten back together, and broken up again with his college girlfriend. Gotten engaged to another woman in Atlanta. And, similarly to Gabby, after a devastating break up, promptly moved to New York. It helped that he'd started his own business and had that flexibility to make a fresh start. Although that hadn't yet included a new woman. To which, he also shared, was the thing his mama asked about every time she called.

"*You're not getting any younger, Dante!*" he mimicked.

"Yes, mama. I know." He shook his head.

"Oh I can relate!" Gabby replied. "*Gabrielle, my dear,*" she also mimicked, "*Time is of the essence!*" She chuckled. "She acts like I'm just working and then sitting at home."

Gabby found it so refreshing to talk to someone else who truly understood this unique plight of approaching 40 and still striking out on the love front. She adored her cousin, Brandy, and, despite the hurdles she'd had, she was in her early 30s, so if it didn't work out with Jalen, she still had years and years ahead of her. And Amaya was her best friend in the world. And even though she'd only been married for 4 years, she'd been with her husband for the past 8.

The flight continued and somewhere over Vegas, Gabby realized how many near misses she and Dante had almost running into each other in the city. She'd mentioned something about attending one of the pier parties at the Wine & Food Festival. He'd been at the same one. He also regularly took classes at the Peloton studios, but their paths hadn't crossed. He'd even spent a random weekend in Bliss Bay this summer, but it was one where she was in the city. And even though they'd found themselves in the same city again for quite some time, the first time they'd come into contact was on a flight to Los Angeles.

As the flight made its descent into Los Angeles, Gabby learned that Dante was planning to visit his best friend from college and his family for the week. He'd put in a few hours of work, but was mostly looking for a chance to rest. Gabby didn't reveal too much, but did mention she was exploring some career options. Shortly after the flight landed, they retrieved their belongings and made their way to the ride share lot where they waited for their respective rides. Their initial plan of riding together was thwarted when they learned they would be heading in opposite directions.

"Sounds like you'll be busy this week, but would love to grab a coffee or something if you have time. Can I get your number?" Dante asked as he held out his phone.

"Of course," Gabby replied as she typed in her number. A minute later, a black sedan pulled up. "Well, there's my ride."

"Gab!" Dante exclaimed as he reached toward Gabrielle and embraced her in a warm hug. "I'm so glad we ran into each other after all this time."

"I can't believe it happened, but I'm so glad, too," Gabby responded, as she soaked in the tenderness of the hug. It had been a while since she had that feeling.

The driver tossed Gabby's bag into the trunk, she hopped in the car, and waved as she said goodbye. As they pulled onto the freeway, Gabby rummaged in her tote bag and pulled out her phone. She smiled at the text that Dante had sent when they exchanged numbers. Then, she opened her text thread with Brandy and Amaya, who knew she was going to L.A. but not exactly why.

"Hey! I arrived. And also, you will NEVER guess what happened!"

What Could Have Been

Brandy and Amaya had rapid fire thoughts and questions.

"No way! What are the odds? Give us the tea!"

"What?! That's wild. What did he look like though? Still fine? I know you said he was fine back in the day."

"Is he single? What's he do?"

"Was there flirting? Oh, and does he live in New York or L.A.?"

Gabby let them know it was, indeed, wild, that he was single, still fine, owned his own business, and lived in New York. *Wait, was he flirting? I don't think so. Just catching up.* She let them know she didn't think there was any flirting.

"Girl, are you sure? You told him you were single, right?"

"That part! Because look at you?! I'm surprised he didn't ask you out!"

That wasn't him asking me out, was it? No! I'm off my game. Gabby shook her head and replied, "I mean. He said coffee if we can figure it out. That's just catching up."

"Gabrielle Giselle Alexander, if you don't go out with this man! I bet there's gonna be a vibe."

"For real. I bet the chemistry is still there 20 years later! You better do drinks instead."

"We'll see. We'll see. Okay. Gotta run!" Gabby cut off the conversation as she pulled up in front of the gorgeous, sleek hotel.

As she settled into her hotel, she thought about what Amaya said. *Would the chemistry still be there?*

She was in such shock on the flight and so focused on the conversation, if there was any, she wouldn't have noticed. But it prompted her to think about that semester in London...

***

Gabby had seen and said hi to Dante in an econ class, but didn't officially meet him until a happy hour hosted by her friend Emiel, from Howard. The ultimate networker, Emiel had managed to meet damn near every Black student studying in London that semester and invited them to the pub. Gabby and Dante chatted over pints and soon became study buddies and friends. Neither of them thought anything of their relationship given they both had significant others back at college. And anytime someone joked around with them about being together all the time, Gabby always retorted, "No! He's like my brother!"

That is until their last week in London.

They'd finished all their exams and were kicking it around town the final few days before they went back to the States. A lot of other friends and students had already left. They had the best time being tourists together hopping on and off the double decker buses.

On their last night, they drank beers at a few pubs and found themselves walking and talking along the Thames on a crisp night under a beautiful full moon. Gabby didn't know if it was the beer, the moon, or the nostalgia of the past few months, but there was a moment where the energy between them shifted. She looked at Dante and felt a magnetic pull. It was like time stopped. She felt compelled to kiss him. But she knew she wouldn't. Couldn't. She had Craig back at school and she loved him and wouldn't put that relationship in jeopardy. She could see in his eyes he had the same realization and they snapped out of the moment and headed back to their respective homes.

They met each other for the tube ride to Heathrow and managed to pretend like the events of the previous evening didn't happen. They amused themselves in the British stores and shops in the airport until it was time for Gabby's flight. Dante walked her to her gate. He held her in a long hug before letting her go. They promised they'd keep in touch, but neither of them ever got around to it and went on with their respective lives. Until this flight crossed their paths again.

While memory lane was fun, for now, she had to focus on her purpose for being in L.A. Making connections for a new job.

Like Old Times

Gabby's week in L.A. was busy, but productive, meeting with potential professional connections. Sushi in Beverly Hills, cocktails in Culver City, and coffee in Santa Monica. She was optimistic about her options as she prepared to head back to New York. Given her schedule, the only time she could meet up with Dante was breakfast before her flight on Friday.

That morning, as she applied her makeup, she FaceTimed with Amaya.

"So, how do you think it's going to go?!" Amaya asked excitedly.

"Fine, I'm sure. I mean, it's breakfast. It's not giving sexy vibes or anything. Just old friends catching up."

"Mmmm hmmm," Amaya replied. "Keep telling yourself that. He is carving time out of his schedule to see you. If he wasn't interested, do you think he would get up early and travel across the city, in that traffic, when he could just see you back in New York?"

Gabby paused. Maybe Amaya was right. But she still didn't know how she felt and didn't want to get in her head before this meetup. She decided to change the subject.

"We shall see. I'll keep you posted. Now where is my BFF?! I miss his little face!" Gabby was referring to Amaya's toddler son, Javier.

"Oh he's napping. And giving Georgia a break!" Georgia was Amaya's adorable dog that Javier gave a run for her money. "He misses Titi Gab! You are overdue for a visit."

"I know, I know. Let me get my life settled and in some kind of order, but soon. I miss you all, too!" She applied a swipe of lip gloss. "Okay, let me go. Love you, Mai."

"Love you too, G."

Gabby hung up the phone, scheduled a pick up, and proceeded to gather her belongings. Shortly after, she found herself in front of Superba Venice where Dante was already waiting for her arrival.

"Hey!" he said, excitedly as he leaned in to hug her.

"Hi!" she replied. It struck her that he smelled the same as he did 20 years ago. Fresh. Clean. Yet warm and familiar. She instantly felt a renewed sense of calm.

Before long, they were chatting over their meals.

"You still love a strong coffee, huh," he gently teased.

"Strong coffee, strong woman!" she replied.

"I'd expect nothing less! How were your meetings this week?"

"Great, actually! Promising. I've been ready for a new professional challenge, so it could be a great fit."

"I'm sure they'd be foolish not to hire you!" He took a sip of coffee. "So you really would move out here? Nothing keeping you in New York?"

"Nope. I guess that's an advantage to the childfree life. Can up and move if you want to," she paused for a bite of bacon. "I mean, my cousin lives there and I love being able to see her all the time. And, she's a little younger and just got serious with someone, so we're also in slightly different places. So, that can be hard."

She surprised herself that she was being quite so honest in the conversation. Dante really had a way of disarming her.

"Yeah. That resonates. I've appreciated it even more this week! I love Cam and his fam, but damn! Those little ones of his," he shook his head and laughed. "They've been giving Uncle Dante a run for his money this week! I'm not built for that full time. I'm good."

So no kids in the plan for you?" she inquired.

"Not in this lifetime! Same for you?" he asked.

"Oh yeah. I've actually known that for a while. I love being Titi Gab and that's enough for me!" she laughed.

The rest of their conversation was effortless and filled with lots of laughs. After about an hour, Dante generously paid for the meal and then offered to take her to the airport. Gabby accepted, realizing she wanted to spend more time with him. She was so drawn to his energy even after all this time.

Dante parked the car at the curb. He got out to open the passenger door for Gabby and then the rear door to take out her bag.

"Well, here you are," he announced.

This time Gabby initiated the hug. "Thank you for breakfast and making time for me." It was in that moment, as his arms wrapped around her, that she felt not just the warmth and sincerity of Dante as a good man and old friend, but potentially something more.

"It was my pleasure. And hey. Let's get up when I'm back in New York."

"For sure."

Gabby grabbed her bag, waved over her shoulder, and then headed to her flight.

We'll See

G abby had planned on weighing her career options and maybe reading a few chapters of her book, but she kept getting distracted with thoughts of Dante.

Did he feel what I felt? Or just the friend vibes? Either way. I'm moving. So what would be the point of even starting something? I don't want a long distance relationship. I don't want another almost right situation. I want right. Real. Every day. Living life together. It's that or nothing. And as daunting as nothing would be I refuse to settle for less.

A few hours later, Gabby landed at JFK. She'd planned ahead and also packed for her last weekend at the beach since she could easily hop on the train from here. It had been a great summer. Very much the one she needed to recover from her breakup. And now, since she'd planned on moving, it would likely be her last weekend here ever. Her plan was to go out with a bang! Figuratively for sure, but after reconnecting with Dante, she didn't know if she had it in her for literally to be an option anymore.

That night she and Brandy stayed in to catch up while the others went out. Brandy poured then each a heavy pour of bubbly.

"Cheers!" Brandy said, clinking their glasses. "Now get to talking!"

Gabby laughed and told Brandy almost everything about the trip. Mostly the parts about Dante since she knew that was what she wanted to hear! She loved seeing Brandy's expressions change with every detail she disclosed. The furrowed eyebrows and puzzled look as she waited to hear his status on wanting children. The "awwws" she let out as she held her hands over her chest when Gabby told her how Dante babysat his friends' kids so they could have a date night. The eyebrows raised in surprise and elation at his desire to see Gabby back in the city. This kept Brandy engaged enough that Gabby didn't have to reveal anything about the work — and potential move — part of the trip.

"Well it sounds promising to me!" Brandy remarked.

"We'll see. He could just be initiating a friendship. Nothing so far has indicated anything else."

"Yeah, but the fact that he drove across town, in all that traffic, just to see you for breakfast...I mean. He could have just waited to see you back in New York. Just because he wasn't trying to jump your bones at the breakfast table doesn't mean he isn't interested! I mean, how cute would this story be at your wedding?!"

"Aren't you skipping a couple of steps, B? We haven't even been on a date yet. Or ever for that matter. Let alone kissed or anything else. Life is not a romance novel! I swear you are getting soft on me. I need you to be a little cynical."

"I'm a changed woman!" Brandy said, smiling with her eyes closed. "But truly, Gab. You have nothing to lose. He seems like a good guy. Maybe just keep the option open. Because as much fun as you've had with these weekend warriors, I don't think any of them are gonna give you what you want long term."

abby paused. "You're right. When did you get so smart little cuz!"

"I learned it by watching you! I just get it now. And to be clear," Brandy said, pausing to take a large sip of her drink. "That doesn't mean you can't close out summer with a little fun. I think Cook Off Chris is here this weekend!" Brandy winked.

"Now that's the B I know! We will see what the weekend holds..." And with that Gabby put their glasses in the sink and retired to bed. She was exhausted.

***

he next day was a typical Saturday at the beach. Sun and fun. Sunset cocktails. Delicious dinner. Ending up at The Sand Dollar. There, across the bar, Gabby spotted Cook off Chris at the same moment he noticed her. Maybe this would take her mind off of whatever was ,or wasn't ,with Dante. He gestured to ask her what she was drinking. She mouthed gin and tonic. He nodded and she saw him place the order with his.

She walked in his direction. As she approached, he handed her the drink

"For you, gorgeous!"

"Thank you!"

"Follow me!" he said, grabbed her hand, and led her across the bar to the photo booth. He sat her on his lap inside the booth. Gabby didn't mind, but she definitely wasn't as hot for him as she was earlier in the summer. He struck her as a bit immature. She knew she wouldn't see him back on the mainland so decided to just go ahead and let him have these make out mini pics for his memories.

As the evening went on, Gabby found herself more annoyed with Chris. When he invited her back to his hot tub (again), she politely declined.

"Maybe another time. I don't feel like getting wet." The truth was there was another kind of wet she wished she could get, but it wasn't going to be from Chris. She decided disrupting her peace and pH balance wasn't worth it.

She decided that for the remaining two days she would just revel in the long, lazy days at the beach and the fun shared meals with her housemates. After Monday, she'd be ready to usher in cooler weather, plan her big move, and focus on finding love in L.A.

She was feeling good. Strong. Confident. And then that all crumbled over Sunday beach cocktails.

Jeremy had just brought down a pitcher of sunset punch as Brandy and Jalen came back holding hands from their walk along the beach. Gabby put down her novel to help fill cups. s Gabby handed Brandy her cup she could see a twinkle in her eye. She held the cup an extra second as Brandy went to take it.

"Something is going on here. What am I missing?" Gabby inquired with a curious look.

"Oh nothingggg," Brandy teased before whispering, "Jalen wants to officially move in together!"

"No way! That's so exciting, B!"

Gabby hugged her cousin. She truly was happy for her. And, in that second after, she felt that familiar tugging at her heart. That duality of being both thrilled for someone else and pained at your own circumstance. She managed to hold it together long enough to finish her drink. She then made a quick escape back up to the house.

She was grateful no one had the bright idea to want to join her.

Behind the closed bathroom door, Gabby released the tears that she'd been holding back. Despite a successful career and a fun, vibrant life, she couldn't help but feel like her shit show of a love life overshadowed it all. She knew what would make her feel better. A purchase! It wasn't a level 10 situation by any means, but maybe a level 5 purchase would do.

She opened her phone to search for her favorite spa downtown. Four p.m. on Tuesday? Click. Done! Even though she would probably have a pile of work on Tuesday, she'd figure it out and work late on Wednesday. She needed the TLC. Next up, dinner. Right as she was scheduling her post spa meal at BONDST, a text message popped up.

t was Dante!

Out on the Town...Twenty Years Later

"Hey Gab. Hope you are enjoying your weekend at the beach. Are you available for dinner tomorrow night? Not sure when you are getting back and what your week looks like."

Her heart pulsated and felt like it might leap through her chest. She decided to take Brandy's advice and stay open to the possibility. Even though in her mind, she was already planning her next chapter, not in New York. She sent off a quick reply.

"Things are great, thanks. And yes. How's 7 pm?" She had originally planned to have a leisurely day at the beach and head back on one of the later ferries, but she was willing to adjust.

While she waited for his return message, she pulled herself together with a rinse of her face.

"Sounds great. How's The Shakespeare? You know. A nod to London."

She felt electricity shoot through her entire body at the thought. "Sounds perfect. See you there."

Just as she was finishing her text, she heard Brandy's voice. "G?! You still in here?

Yeah. I'm here!" She gave herself a once over in the mirror and left the bathroom. "Hey!" she said as she emerged.

"Hey. You'd been gone for a minute. Wanted to make sure you were all good."

"Yeah. All good."

"What are you not telling me?"

"Oh nothinggggggg," she replied, mimicking Brandy's earlier statement. "Just seeing Dante tomorrow."

"G! That's exciting! See!"

"We'll see," Gabby replied.

Gabby could hardly wait for the next day and committed to being present for her last weekend at the beach. Though every once in a while her mind would drift to what she was planning to wear or what the vibe might be with Dante in that setting.

***

The next night, Gabby found herself in front of The Shakespeare in an emerald green silk dress, loose curls bouncing on her shoulder, feeling beautiful, confident, and ready for a fun evening. Dante was already waiting inside the restaurant when she arrived.

They had another magical meal together. It felt even more special that it brought back memories of their time abroad. Since neither of them was quite ready to say goodbye after dinner, they walked a bit through Bryant Park. There was a chill in the air and Dante offered Gabby his jacket. As she thanked him, she noticed just how full the moon was and it instantly transported her back to that moment along the Thames and that same compulsion she felt to kiss him was back. At least this time there was no boyfriend back home to stop her! She wondered if he had the same thought because she saw something shift in his eyes. And before she knew it, he was leaning in to kiss her.

It was magical! She felt like she was in one of those damn rom coms that Amaya loved! *Was there music playing? Were there birds chirping? Had time stopped?* In actuality, none of that had happened, but it felt like it could have.

"I've been waiting to do that for twenty years," Dante stated as they unlocked lips.

"Yeah," Gabby softly replied. "Me too."

After some more kissing in the park, Dante put Gabby in a cab home. It was a school night after all and he knew Gabby had a busy day ahead after all the travel. But this was not without securing time on her calendar for Friday night.

Gabby was on cloud nine and wanted to share this update with Amaya and Brandy, but decided to do that tomorrow. She wanted to bask in this glow by herself a little bit longer.

At Last

Gabby eventually told Amaya and Brandy about the romantic evening and the subsequent plan for Friday night. It was the main topic of the text thread all week. But despite how exciting everything was, Gabby still was a bit hesitant as she expected to hear about one of the L.A. jobs very soon. And nothing, not even a man, was going to keep her from pursuing her career goals.

Friday was fabulous. Dinner and then drinks at a jazz club where Dante's friend was playing. Since they were making up for lost time, Gabby planned a Sunday afternoon museum trip that turned into drinks, dinner, and a nightcap. The following Thursday, Dante invited Gabby over to cook dinner for her.

Her text messages were on fire that day! Interspersed with her work was a lot of laughing at "get it, girl" memes from Amaya and Brandy.

"What are you going to wear?! It better be hot! And whatever is underneath better be too, because you know tonight is going to be the night!" Brandy shared.

"Girl. Are you ready ready? I hope you were able to squeeze in a wax!" Amaya inquired.

he arrived at Dante's place with a bottle of bubbly and a bottle of red, freshly waxed, wearing a simple, but sexy, body hugging dress in royal blue, which she knew happened to be Dante's favorite color.

"Wow!" he exclaimed as he opened the door to his place and took in the beauty in front of him.

hey had another tantalizing evening. For Gabby, it was as if every sense was heightened. After a delicious homemade meal and a delectable dessert, they found themselves on the couch, each with a glass of wine, listening to Marvin Gaye. That lasted about 2twentyminutes.

hen both of their glasses were empty, rather than take them to the kitchen and disrupt the mood, Dante leaned over and planted a soft kiss on Gabby's lips. She kissed back with a hunger that only comes with years of yearning. She couldn't help but find herself with her dress hiked up around her waist straddling Dante on the couch. Her mouth found its way to his neck where she lightly nibbled. He let out a guttural moan. He gently grabbed her hair and pulled her away only for him to return the favor. She instinctively arched her back to further expose her neck to provide him greater access. It wasn't enough for her. She knew she wanted him and was more than happy to take control. She tugged at the hem of her dress and pulled the stretchy fabric up and over her head revealing her naked breasts and thong. She tossed the garment somewhere behind her. Dante was very obviously pleased, as she could see, and feel. In response, she motioned her head toward the bedroom asking if he'd like to take the party there. And in one fell swoop, he picked her up and carried her toward his room and his bed where both of their desires took over.

The next morning, light streamed in from the window glistening on their post coital faces cuddled up in the bed. Gabby was awakened by a light kiss on her lips.

"Good morning," Dante whispered.

"Morning!" Gabby whispered back as she stretched. Out of the corner of her eye she spotted the clock and realized that she could not stay here all day. She allowed herself to lay there another minute before sitting up in bed.

"Don't go!" Dante half teased, half pleaded.

"I wish I didn't have to," she said, begrudgingly as she gave him another kiss before standing up. She didn't miss the fact that Dante's eyebrows raised as he admired her naked body.

After using the bathroom and rinsing her face, she found her way back in the living room where she pondered pulling her dress back on. She chuckled to herself at the thought of doing a walk of shame at her big age. *Whatever! They can be jealous! Because that was worth it!*

When she looked up, there was Dante holding a t-shirt and some sweatpants. "You wanna wear this home?"

"Yeah. It will probably be more comfortable than this," she said, holding up her dress.

"I mean...it looked amazing on you...and on my floor," Dante replied.

That comment alone elicited a stirring in Gabby's nether regions. She really had to go. She walked toward him to retrieve the clothing.

"So...when can I get these back?" he asked with a wink.

"Soon. Very soon!" she replied as she pulled on the items. She gave him a quick kiss on the lips. "Have to hustle to get on this work call, but I'll text you later."

Now What?

G abby hustled home in a cab and went about her busy day of work. She managed to squeeze in a shower and a quick text exchange with the girls. She was grateful it was a remote work day for her.

Around 3 p.m., her phone rang. It was one of the firms from L.A. offering her a job with a very appealing salary and benefits package. She told them she would follow up on Monday after she had time to consider the offer. But she knew it was an amazing opportunity and what she wanted for her next chapter.

However, after she hung up, reality hit her. Yes, this was everything she wanted for her career and she was excited about moving to a new city. And, what would that mean for her and Dante? It couldn't have been a coincidence that they reconnected and *reconnected* after all these years. But she knew she didn't have it in her to do long distance. That wouldn't be fair to either of them. She resigned herself to the fact that she would chalk the last couple weeks up to an incredible experience she would remember forever. She'd pack it away, pack up her stuff, and have a fresh start in L.A. After all, there were tons of men there, too, right?

But now what? He was expecting to see her. And she did want to see him again, but would it be too hard to face the truth?

She needed input from the girls. Which meant she also needed to break this news to Brandy. She picked up her phone and gave her a call.

"G!" Brandy answered, "What's up? You never call. What's going on? Is there another Level 10 situation happening?!"

"Oh no! Quite the opposite actually. I have some great news to share!"

"Well, what now? I already know you had a very *stimulating* evening with Dante," Brandy replied using her dramatic, soap opera voice.

"Girl yes! But that's not it. So...there's something I didn't tell you about the trip to L.A..."

"Ummm, okay. Continue..."

"So, I was actually out there looking for a new job. And today, I got a really amazing offer. And I think I'm going to take it!"

"OMG! That's amazing! I'm so proud of you. Any place would be lucky to have you. But damn. I'm going to miss you, cousin!"

"I know. You've been the best part of living here, B. It will be an adjustment, but I'm really ready for the change."

I hear that. Shit. If I hadn't met Jalen, I'd probably be right behind you. So wait. What does this mean for you and Dante?"

"Well, that's the question. I haven't told him yet. But it's so early. I think I may just need to let it be the fun moment it was and move on. If neither of us are with anyone and he happens to be in L.A. visiting...you know. Maybe a little reunion. But I don't see how it can be more than that."

Brandy was quiet.

"You're quiet. What's that about?" Gabby asked.

I don't know, G. Maybe it's naive of me, but what if this is it? Seriously. What are the odds you'd find each other again? And yes, it was fun and sexy, but that wasn't all you mentioned. There was something different in your voice when you talked about him. Something deeper. Because before anything even happened, everything you mentioned was about how good of a person he is. How he cares about his friends and family. How he remembered all these things about you."

Gabby sighed. "Yeah…maybe you're right. But long distance? Ugh. I just want a man in my same damn city."

"That would be something to figure out. But I wouldn't throw away the whole idea. For what it's worth. Life is short and something special is hard to find!

You really are a smart one Brandy Camille Bowman!"

"Not my full government name! But yes. I've learned a few things. Good luck and keep me posted! You'll end up where you're meant to be. I just know it!"

Gabby hung up the phone. She decided to put on her big girl pants and send a text to Dante.

Make a Wish

Later that evening, Gabby heard her buzzer ring. A moment later, Dante was at her door.

Hey," she said softly as she opened the door and saw him, in all his handsome glory, standing there. She greeted him with a tender hug.

"Hey!" he replied, excitedly. "I didn't think I'd be getting my clothes back this quickly!" he joked.

He followed her through her apartment and to her couch where she already had two glasses of wine poured.

"What's going on?' he asked. "It sounded urgent."

"Well, it kind of is." She took a large sip of her wine. "I'm just going to come out and say it."

Dante looked at her expectantly.

"So, the past couple of weeks have been amazing! The fact that after all these years we've crossed paths again is nothing short of incredible. And it looks like, yet again, timing isn't on our side. I've been offered an incredible job in L.A. and I'm going to take it."

"Well, congratulations," he said without flinching. "And cheers! That's really incredible, Gabby."

"Thanks." She wondered if maybe she'd mis-read this situation. And that he only saw this as a fun thing so it wouldn't be a big deal for him that she was leaving. She was crestfallen. She bit the inside of her lip to hold back what felt like tears forming.

At that moment, Dante said, "Wait. What's up? I know it's been 20 years, but I can tell some-thing is off." He reached out and held her hand in his.

She was touched. And confused! He was everything she wanted. And yet, she had to say goodbye. "Well, what does that mean for...us?" She looked up at him and into his eyes.

"Gab, I don't want to lose you again. I don't think it's a mistake that we found each other again and at a time where we are both single. I don't know. Maybe I'm crazy, but life is too short to let a good thing go. It doesn't make any sense, but I'd be willing to try."

"I appreciate that. And I *really* want to. But I'm just not sure I can do the long distance thing."

"I hear that. How about this? Let's make a deal. Give me a couple of months to get things in order here. If things are still good, I'll move."

Gabby was speechless as she tried to process what she was hearing. A beat later, she replied, "You would?"

"I would. I believe in us and I'm willing to make it work."

Gabby reached out and pulled Dante into a big hug. "Okay. Let's do it."

***

Four months later, it was Gabby's 40th birthday. After a half day at work, she went to her new favorite spa for a massage. She felt renewed as she pulled on a gorgeous emerald jumpsuit and applied a little makeup for her night out. As she looked back at her reflection in the mirror, she smiled. She was so proud of how far she'd come in the past year. She couldn't have imagined all the amazing things the Universe had in store for her and she paused for a moment of gratitude.

An hour later she found herself looking across the table into Dante's eyes, their fingers interlocked. While the view at Nobu was stunning, nothing compared to looking deeply into the eyes of her love. He had just moved to L.A. last week and she couldn't be happier! At the end of her meal, her dessert arrived with a lit candle celebrating her big day.

Dante exclaimed, "Make a wish, babe!"

As she stared at the flame, she glowed with joy realizing that all of her wishes had already come true.

Epilogue

Ellerie

D*eet deet deet deet deet.*

Deet deet deet deet deet.

Deet deet deet deet deet.

Ellerie heard the familiar sounds of FaceTime emerging from her crossbody bag as she softly shut the door to Noah's place behind her. She'd fallen into the fellow expat's bed more than a few times during her time in Mexico City. Was it the fun they had or the fact that he lived closer to Panadería Rosetta? Maybe both.

As she walked down the flight of steps, she unzipped her bag and saw it was both of her brothers calling. She rummaged in the bag to find her AirPods and to take the call.

Dammit!

She fumbled with her technology still being taunted by the *deet deet deet deet deet* of the call.

"Okay! Okay!" she said out loud to herself as she prepared to make the connection. She caught a quick glimpse of herself back on the screen, braids piled messily atop her head with only a sweep of lip balm.

Well, not my finest look.

In the light of the morning, she managed to put aside any creeping intrusive thoughts about the wrinkles she saw starting to form around her eyes and the slight dullness in her skin, only noticeable to her. She was naturally pretty, but the whole turning 40 thing activated her slightest insecurities.

"Hello?" she answered, as she stepped onto the street and slid on her sunglasses.

"Hey big sis!" Jalen exclaimed.

"Hi Ellerie!" his sweet girlfriend, Brandy, said with a wave.

"You never called me back," her twin, Ellis stated.

"Well hello to you, too, Ellis," Ellerie retorted. "Hey, J!" she replied sweetly. These brothers of hers instantly took her back to their exact childhood dynamics. She and Ellis at each other for something, and feeling only fondness for sweet baby brother, Jalen.

"Hi Brandy! Don't you look happy!" Brandy was always a cheerful girl from what Ellerie knew, but she was especially giddy right now, considering how early it was on a Sunday morning.

"I am!" Brandy gave Jalen the googly eyes.

"Well, since we're all here..." Jalen started.

"Finally..." Ellis mumbled. Ellerie narrowed her eyes at him behind her sunnies.

"Well. We have some news," Jalen continued. Then looked at Brandy, who could no longer contain herself.

"We're engaged!!!" She then immediately thrust her left hand into the camera and showed off the glistening diamond on her ring finger.

Ellerie was flooded with a range of emotions, but the deep love she had for her baby brother and the elation she had at his happiness took over first.

"Congratulations! I'm so happy for you both. Awww. J!!!" she teared up.

Ellis, who never had a poker face, was clearly shocked, but also activated his happiness for his brother. "My man. I'm proud of you, dude. Congrats! You did well. And we can't wait to welcome you to the family, Brandy."

"Thanks, y'all. It means a lot." Jalen responded, beaming with pride at the admiration of his siblings. "Well, we have a few other calls to make and then both sets of parents are driving up for brunch."

"Oh my. I hope your mother behaves." Ellerie responded. They all deeply loved their mama, but she could be...a lot. Especially since this might finally lead to the grandbabies she so desperately wanted. "And, I want to hear all the details when you have time! Call me later this week."

"I will. And when will you be back? I want us to all celebrate in person."

Before she could respond, Brandy jumped in. "And yes, I want you to be in the wedding so we have lots to talk about, too!"

"Soon," was all she could reply as she approached her turn on to the street, *Colima*. She could feel the tide turning and her other emotions welling up inside her body. She had to get off the call. This was far too much to absorb on a Sunday morning before coffee. "Okay. Enjoy! Love you all. Bye!"

"*Hola. ¿Cómo estás? Tengo un americano y...una concha y...chocolatín.*" Despite the lump in her throat, she eked out her order, and then, luckily, managed to find a seat. *I guess being Ellerie, party of one, is good for something.*

"*Gracias*," she replied to the server as her meal was placed in front of her.

As she took a long sip of her americano and a big bite of her pastry, she sighed. The gravity of it all — her baby brother's engagement, how she ended up in Mexico City, and the uncertainty of what was to come, was a lot. Everything in her life felt off its axis. Jumbled. Confusing. She knew she had some things to figure out, but for now she was going to just eat her feelings.

Thank You

Thank you for reading *Gabby: A Bliss Bay Romance*! If you enjoyed this book, I would be grateful if you could leave a review. Reviews help boost book sales. As an indie author, they are especially helpful!

Thank you!

Kayla

Bliss Bay Series

Want more from Bliss Bay? Buy book 1, *Brandy*, and book 2, *Danielle*. Plus other fun bonus content at Give them Romance https://www.give themromance.com/

About the Author

Kayla Love has been writing since she could put a pen in her hand. While she's mostly written non-fiction, she's excited to venture into the Bliss Bay series as her first works of fiction. Her goal is to write compelling, fun, and real romance stories that reflect the diverse experiences of Black women like herself and the other the women of color in her world. Many of her characters and storylines are inspired by her time living in New York, including numerous summers at the beach.

Like her character, Brandy, Kayla was born and bred in New Jersey, loves spending time at the beach, eating bacon, and drinking black coffee and Cabernet Franc. A founding Corner of Press author, Kayla now resides in California.

www.ingramcontent.com/pod-product-compliance
Lightning Source LLC
Chambersburg PA
CBHW060336310726
48976CB00007B/2581